AN ELEGANT WEAPON

With the press of a button, the cylinder-shaped metal hilt releases a brilliant shaft of energy in a sizzling *snap-hiss*. Stopping about a meter from the dish-like emitter, the humming beam of energy appears as a solid, bright core of light radiating a haze of color.

No weapon is more instantly recognizable as a symbol of the Jedi Order than the lightsaber. For over a thousand generations, Jedi Knights have carried these elegant energy blades in their quest to protect peace and justice in the Galactic Republic. The Sith, a dark offshoot of the Jedi, also wield lightsabers. However, in the hands of a Sith, a lightsaber is used for attack, domination, and execution rather than for defense. Only a Jedi Knight can wield a lightsaber to its full potential.

A Brief History

Over 25,000 years ago, at the start of the Galactic Republic, the Jedi Order began as a group of Force-users on the world of Tython. They carried metal blades, honed through the Force to have supernatural strength and sharpness. In time, early Jedi applied off-world technology and replaced their physical blades with ones made of energy, creating the first true lightsabers.

The lightsaber has changed little since it was created, but the Jedi Order has grown and groups have split from the Order. With these new groups, variations on lightsaber design evolved and these can be found all over the galaxy.

ANATOMY OF A LIGHTSABER

Lightsaber handles, or hilts, are usually about 30 centimeters long—although some hilts are longer and some are less than half this length. Whatever they may look like on the outside, most lightsabers contain the same technology inside.

The **energy cell** unleashes its power through the **primary crystal**. When building a lightsaber, a Jedi must use the Force to carefully line up the energy cell with the primary crystal. A true lightsaber cannot be assembled by a machine. Only those sensitive to the Force can construct one.

A separate **focusing crystal** concentrates the released energy into a beam. This gem gives the beam its color and its unique "feel"—characteristics that determine how it moves and vibrates.

Once the energy is focused, it leaves the handle through a positively charged **energy lens** inside the **blade emitter**. After about a meter, the beam bends back toward the hilt and passes through a negatively charged high-energy flux aperture, also in the blade emitter. To an observer, it looks like the blade simply stops growing, but this loop of energy creates the lightsaber's distinctive hum as well as the spinning effect in the blade's movements, which makes the weapon difficult to control for those without training.

As the beam, or blade, loops back into the handle, a **superconductor** channels the energy back to the power cell. As a result, a lightsaber is extremely energy efficient; it uses all its power at once and yet never loses any.

There are legends about ancient lightsabers that required battery packs strapped to utility belts or worn as backpacks. A thick conducting cable connected the battery to the hilt. Few examples of such relics have survived.

STAR WARS

LIGHTSABERS

A GUIDE TO WEAPONS OF THE FORCE

Written by Pablo Hidalgo

SCHOLASTIC

SCHOLASTIC

www.scholastic.com

Published by Scholastic Inc., 557 Broadway, New York, NY 10012
Scholastic Canada Ltd., Markham Ontario; Scholastic UK Ltd.,
Southam Warwickshire

Scholastic and associated logos are trademarks of Scholastic Inc.

Produced by becker&mayer!, LLC.
11120 NE 33rd Place, Suite 101
Bellevue, WA 98004
www.beckermayer.com

becker&mayer!
BOOK PRODUCERS

If you have questions or comments about this product, please visit
www.beckermayer.com/customerservice.html and click on the
Customer Service Request Form.

Written by Pablo Hidalgo
Edited by Delia Greve
Designed by Rosanna Brockley
Design assistance by Sarah Baynes and Cortny Helmick
Production management by Larry Weiner

Illustrations page 6 (Obi-Wan Kenobi lightsaber construction,
bondar and solari crystals) by Chris Reiff.
Illustrations pages 5-6 (Skywalker cutaway lightsaber, kasha and
kathracite crystal) by Chris Trevas.

06/10 Dongguang, China

Printed, manufactured, and assembled in China

10 9 8 7 6 5 4 3 2 1

ISBN 978-0-545-27177-6

09390

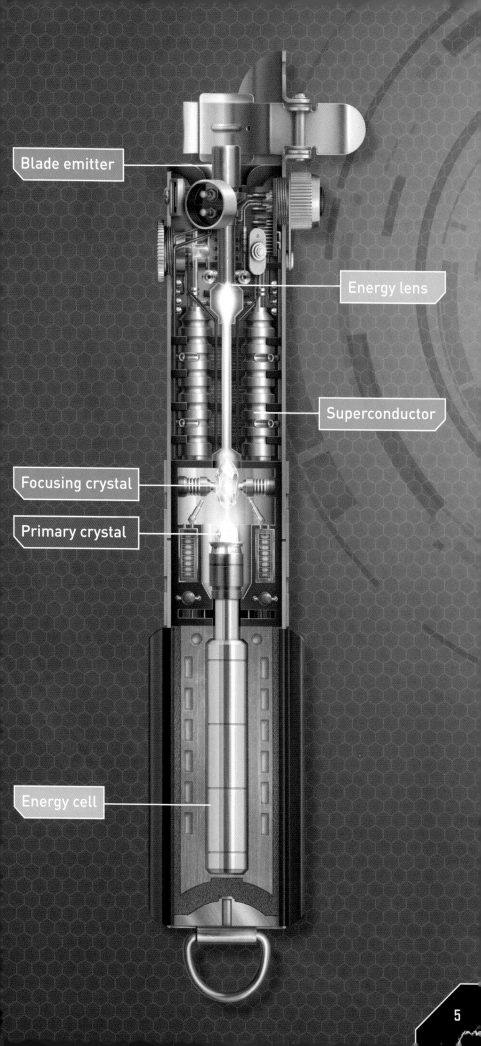

Blade emitter

Energy lens

Superconductor

Focusing crystal

Primary crystal

Energy cell

5

BUILDING A LIGHTSABER

As a part of Jedi tradition, each Padawan must construct his or her own lightsaber during training. First the Padawan learns to construct the handle, and then to harvest what will become the focusing crystal at the center of the weapon. The entire construction typically takes a month; however, in times of crisis, trained Jedi Knights and Masters have been known to build a lightsaber in as little time as a day.

Selecting a Crystal

The focusing crystal in a Jedi lightsaber is usually collected from the sacred Jedi cavern on the snowy world of Ilum. However, other jewels have been used throughout Jedi history with varying effectiveness.

Kathracite produces a weaker blade.

Bondar crystals create a dull blade so it has a stunning sting rather than a lethal edge.

Solari crystals widen the width of a blade, making blaster deflection easier.

Kasha crystals, which come from Cerean, are said to aid in meditation and Force attunement.

Lightsaber Assembly

A Jedi forges the connection between the crystal and the power source through a concentrated application of the Force. To do so, a Jedi enters a trancelike state of meditation, in which he or she feels and responds to the unique call of the crystal.

Tuning a Lightsaber

A lightsaber is an extension of a Jedi's Force awareness. Because Jedi let the Force guide their selection of the crystal, the vibration the crystal creates in the lightsaber blade helps Jedi center themselves and find balance in the Force. In this way, a Jedi can center his or her attention beyond the distractions of combat.

EXOTIC LIGHTSABERS

- The **shoto** is a more compact version of a lightsaber with a shorter blade, used primarily as a defensive guard by those who carry two lightsabers.

- A **guard shoto** is attached to a regular lightsaber hilt at a 90-degree angle, allowing the blade to be held parallel to the forearm and spun in a complex form of defense or attack.

- The **dual-phase lightsaber** contains multiple crystals that allow its blade length to be extended or shortened mid-combat.

- One of the rarest offshoots of lightsaber technology is the **lightwhip**, which can consist of snake-like energy tendrils and physical metallic lashes, forming a weapon that can both slice and trap an opponent.

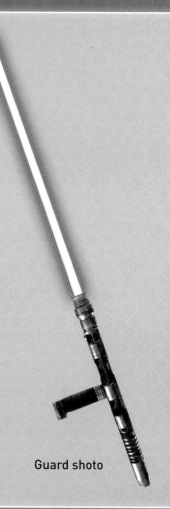

Guard shoto

SITH SABERS

A Sith lightsaber is constructed using similar methods, but the underlying philosophy is quite different. Jedi let the Force flow through them, allowing it to guide their actions. Sith, on the other hand, focus their anger and hate to mold their device. Sith prefer using synthetic or artificial crystals they craft. To do this, they melt a variety of minerals into acids, which are reformed as a crystalline solid inside a pressurized furnace. A Sith Lord helps shape the crystal in the furnace by concentrating on his or her anger and the dark side of the Force.

A Jedi's connection to his or her lightsaber is a powerful bond, but not one of emotional attachment. It takes a lifetime for Jedi to achieve true mastery of their handcrafted weapons. In this way, Jedi form a keen sense for the nuances, or "feel," of their lightsabers.

Lightsabers have few moving parts, which make them quite rugged. They can operate in the frigid temperatures of space or in the scorching heat of a fiery world. Nonetheless, the components of a lightsaber can be susceptible to the elements, and a Jedi must take special care of his or her weapon. There are a few rules a Jedi would do well to remember.

Basic Guidelines

1. Standard lightsabers and water don't mix.
While some protective measures exist, such as flashback waterseals, igniting a lightsaber underwater can be a problem. The weapon may boil the surrounding water, adding a spinning turbulence in the blade's path and making it difficult to control. Should a Jedi submerge into water through the course of an assignment, he or she had best make sure the lightsaber's power is deactivated.

2. Maintain proper alignment.
Care must be taken to ensure the focusing crystal remains in the proper position. A damaged crystal could cause the blade's energy to destabilize and the power cell to explode.

3. Guard your lightsaber.
Above all, Jedi must keep track of their lightsabers. Should a lightsaber fall into the hands of an unpracticed or dishonorable person, it will almost always lead to tragedy.

A Jedi who loses a lightsaber often builds another. In times of great need—such as the emergency of the Clone Wars—the Order keeps replacement lightsabers ready for Jedi to use while they build a new one.

MYTH
Only a Jedi or a Sith can wield a lightsaber.

FACT
Anyone can conceivably pick up a lightsaber and use it, but sabers are extremely difficult to wield. Those used to swinging solid swords often find using a weightless blade a challenge—one that can have dangerous consequences. Only through rigorous training and enhanced senses through the Force can a Jedi use a lightsaber to its full potential.

OBI-WAN KENOBI

Notes

Obi-Wan Kenobi built this lightsaber
as a Padawan to resemble that of his
mentor, Qui-Gon Jinn, as a show of
respect. Obi-Wan lost this lightsaber
on Naboo when Darth Maul kicked it
into a smelting pit. He rebuilt an exact
replica that he used until the start of
the Clone Wars, when it was taken by
the Geonosians. Obi-Wan then created a
new design. (See pages 44–45.)

The blade emitter is not covered or protected; instead, it is a flat projection plate.

Hilt Length:
28.00 centimeters (11.00")

Hilt Width:
5.00 centimeters (2.00")

Material:
Alloy metal

Blade Color:
Blue

Focusing Crystal:
Single Adegan crystal

The scalloped handgrip lets Obi-Wan command a firm grasp of his weapon.

Hilt Length:
28.50 centimeters (11.25")

Hilt Width:
3.80 centimeters (1.50")

Material:
Alloy metal

Blade Color:
Green

Focusing Crystal:
Single Adegan crystal

The ridged handgrip contains a series of micro-power cells, which enables more control over the lightsaber's current charge levels.

Notes

Qui-Gon Jinn's lightsaber may not be as ornate as that of his mentor, Count Dooku, but true to his rebellious ways, he used it to master the same classical fighting techniques as well as untraditional combat forms from across the galaxy. After Qui-Gon's death, Obi-Wan briefly used this lightsaber to kill Darth Maul. It is now kept in a memorial within the Jedi Temple.

YODA

Notes

With a stooped, small appearance, Yoda may not look like a great warrior, but his skills with a lightsaber were unequaled. Rather than carry his weapon on his belt, Yoda concealed it within the fabric around his waist. During his battle with Darth Sidious, Yoda lost this weapon inside the massive Galactic Senate chamber.

Yoda's lightsaber is small in comparison with the lightsabers of other Jedi. It is similar to a shoto blade used by some specialists.

Hilt Length:
14.00 centimeters (5.50")

Hilt Width:
2.80 centimeters (1.13")

Material:
Alloy metal

Blade Color:
Green

Focusing Crystal:
Single Adegan crystal

DARTH MAUL

Notes

Darth Maul based the design of his double-bladed lightsaber on ancient plans found deep within a Sith Holocron owned by Darth Sidious. Eager to destroy the Jedi, Darth Maul felt a single-bladed weapon was far too limiting.

Hilt Length:
49.50 centimeters (19.50")

Hilt Width:
4.40 centimeters (1.75")

Material:
Alloy metal

Blade Color:
Red

Focusing Crystal:
Four synthetic crystals

Functioning as a saberstaff, Darth Maul's weapon consists of two lightsabers fused together so the blades extend in a single line. Each blade can be ignited separately, depending on the situation and the opponent being faced.

This precisely crafted, tapered hilt is covered with a gleaming electrum-plated finish—a decoration allowed only for senior Jedi Council members. Besides its uniquely crafted exterior, this lightsaber is also noted for its purple blade.

Hilt Length:
28.00 centimeters (11.00")

Hilt Width:
6.35 centimeters (2.50")

Material:
Electrum-plated alloy

Blade Color:
Purple

Focusing Crystal:
Single Hurikane amethyst

Notes

Mace Windu carried several lightsabers in his long career, but this last one was the most remarkable. Legends say the focusing gem was harvested from a remote world inhabited by living crystal aliens. The midsection unscrews to allow easy access to the central crystal chamber. Windu used this lightsaber to dispatch Jango Fett, creating an enemy in his son, young Boba Fett.

KI-ADI-MUNDI

Notes

As a species, Cereans prefer low-tech
culture. Though Ki-Adi-Mundi was
comfortable with modern technology, he
still admired the simpler Cerean ways.
He purposely designed his lightsaber
hilt without frills or accents. During his
meditation, Ki-Adi-Mundi's dual, or binary,
brain bonded with two crystals. Thus his
lightsaber carries both.

The ridges along the upper half of the handle allow for a firm two-handed grip.

Hilt Length:
26.60 centimeters (10.50")

Hilt Width:
4.50 centimeters (1.80")

Material:
Durasteel

Blade Color:
Blue or green

Focusing Crystal:
Variable blue and green Adegan crystals

Hilt Length:
28.00 centimeters (11.00")

Hilt Width:
5.00 centimeters (2.00")

Material:
Alloy metal

Blade Color:
Blue

Focusing Crystal:
Single Adegan crystal

This rugged lightsaber design is noted for the radiator casing segment, which forms the tapered, or conical, shape at the base of the hilt.

PLO KOON

Notes

Using historical texts found within the Jedi archives, Plo Koon, along with several fellow Jedi Knights, designed this hilt to resemble the lightsaber carried by Lacunas Subartuk, one of the most vigilant Jedi of the ancient Order. In future generations, this design would inspire the more modern "Sentinel" lightsaber hilt in the Jedi Order founded by Luke Skywalker.

KIT FISTO

Notes

Being from an aquatic species native to the waters of Glee Anselm, Kit Fisto modified his lightsaber so the beam could energize even when fully submerged in water. To achieve this, he used two crystals charged by an ignition pulse that is split into two currents. Fisto's customized modification proved popular among the Order, especially during the Clone Wars when action brought Jedi to such watery planets as Kamino.

The blade emitter is widened to support twin crystals.

Integral flashback waterseals built into the hilt allow this lightsaber to ignite underwater.

Hilt Length:
26.60 centimeters (10.50")

Hilt Width:
3.80 centimeters (1.50")

Material:
Alloy metal

Blade Color:
Green

Focusing Crystal:
Paired Adegan crystals

The elegant curved handle design along with its flourishing blade-emitter guard makes this lightsaber hilt distinct. It also contains a reserve power cell at its base.

Hilt Length:
35.50 centimeters (14.00")

Hilt Width:
7.60 centimeters (3.00")

Material:
Alloy metal

Blade Color:
Red

Focusing Crystal:
Synthetic Sith crystal

COUNT DOOKU
(A.K.A. DARTH TYRANUS)

Notes

This notable design departs from Jedi tradition, but the curved hilt perfectly suited the classic form of lightsaber combat Count Dooku perfected. He replaced his original blue Adegan crystal with a synthetic red Sith gem when he took the title Darth Tyranus. Though Dooku turned his back on the Jedi traditions, he still greeted his opponents with the customary salute of a Jedi when engaging in duels.

LIGHTSABER

Notes

Jedi initiates—students who have yet to be paired into Padawan-Master relationships—begin training with lightsabers at a very young age: three or four years old for humans. Training lightsabers emit low-intensity blades that cannot cut and are not lethal. Contact with a training blade will only sting or numb an opponent; however, these blades do convey an accurate sensation of holding a real lightsaber.

Training lightsabers are smaller than standard lightsabers, built for the small hands of Jedi initiates.

Hilt Length:
Varies, but typically 16.50 centimeters (6.50")

Hilt Width:
Varies, but typically 2.50 centimeters (1.00")

Material:
Durasteel, copper, and tempered plastics

Blade Color:
Blue or green

Focusing Crystal:
Single Adegan crystal shard

Hilt Length:
28.00 centimeters (11.00")

Hilt Width:
5.00 centimeters (2.00")

Material:
Alloy metal

Blade Color:
Green

Focusing Crystal:
Single Adegan crystal

Like that of Plo Koon's lightsaber, this hilt features a conical radiator casing segment at the base. However, this hilt includes a manganese brass casing at the base, a treatment that prevents corrosion.

LUMINARA UNDULI

Notes

A serious-minded Jedi Master, Luminara studied many Jedi traditions and found inspiration in molding her lightsaber after that of one of the greatest Jedi warriors. Luminara's Mirialan heritage made her incredibly agile and flexible, qualities she used to the fullest when engaging in lightsaber combat.

ANAKIN SKYWALKER

Notes

Anakin Skywalker had visions of the dark side while in his trance-like state in the sacred caverns of Ilum, where he meditated on the construction of this lightsaber. The weapon is in contrast to the delicate saber design of his mentor, Obi-Wan Kenobi. Anakin built his lightsaber instead for maximum power. However, he lost this lightsaber just prior to the Clone Wars when factory equipment on Geonosis cut the handle in two.

Notes

Generally, someone incapable of using the Force would find wielding a lightsaber difficult. However, the advanced technology built into Grievous's mechanical body gave him supernaturally fast reflexes and coordination. He could also split his two arms into four, letting him wield four lightsabers at a time.

While Grievous kept a grim trophy room in his hidden lair and carried many stolen lightsabers in the lining of his cape, these four lightsabers were his greatest prizes.

Previous Owner: Pablo-Jill
Hilt Length: 29.20 centimeters (11.40")
Hilt Width: 6.65 centimeters (2.60")
Material: Alloy metal
Blade Color: Blue
Focusing Crystal: Single Adegan crystal

Previous Owner: Adi Gallia
Hilt Length: 26.60 centimeters (10.50")
Hilt Width: 3.30 centimeters (1.30")
Material: Durasteel
Blade Color: Green
Focusing Crystal: Single Adegan crystal

Grievous claimed Pablo-Jill's lightsaber from floating debris, after Grievous injured him during an intense duel in a collapsing satellite city over Duro.

During a Clone Wars battle on Boz Pity, General Grievous overpowered Master Gallia with his multiple arms, striking her down and claiming her lightsaber.

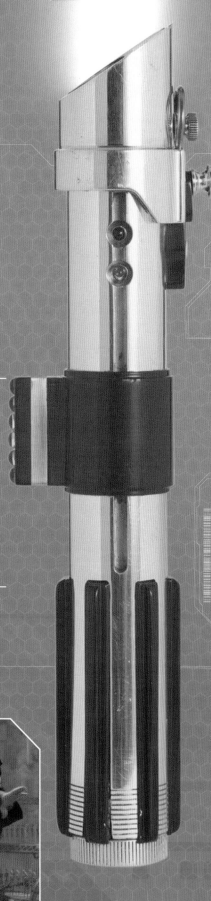

The thick cylinder shape along with the contrasting alloy and carbon gives this lightsaber a blunt, imposing profile.

Hilt Length:
25.40 centimeters (10.00")

Hilt Width:
3.00 centimeters (1.20")

Material:
Alloy metal and carbon composites

Blade Color:
Blue

Focusing Crystal:
Single Adegan crystal

ious Owner: Roron Corobb
Length: 26.80 centimeters (10.50")
Width: 4.30 centimeters (1.70")
erial: Alloy metal
e Color: Green
sing Crystal: Single Adegan crystal

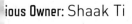

ious Owner: Shaak Ti
Length: 26.60 centimeters (10.50")
Width: 3.30 centimeters (1.30")
erial: Copper and durasteel
e Color: Blue
sing Crystal: Single Adegan crystal

When General Grievous stormed the Republic capital, he cut through layers of security forces and Jedi protectors including Corobb. He was killed by Grievous defending Chancellor Palpatine.

Pre
Hilt
Hil
Ma
Bla
Foc

Pr
Hilt
Hilt
Ma
Bla
Fo

As the last line of defense for Chancellor Palpatine, in a final battle of the Clone Wars, Grievous ensnared Shaak Ti with electrified cables, which knocked her unconscious and allowed Grievous to steal her lightsaber.

AAYLA SECURA

Notes

Aayla Secura's extended assignments on frontier worlds with her Master, Quinlan Vos, often kept her far from Coruscant. As such, she chose to construct a functional weapon that allowed for easy maintenance and upkeep. Unable to rely on the resources of the Jedi Temple when in the field, Aayla made do with common tool kits to keep her lightsaber maintained.

This hilt is noted as much for its common, simplistic design as it is for the threaded handgrip on the upper half of the handle.

Hilt Length:
26.60 centimeters (10.50")

Hilt Width:
4.50 centimeters (1.80")

Material:
Durasteel

Blade Color:
Blue

Focusing Crystal:
Single Adegan crystal

The threaded section at the center of the hilt allows for a balanced grip for those favoring a single-handed fighting style.

Hilt Length:
26.60 centimeters (10.50")

Hilt Width:
3.80 centimeters (1.50")

Material:
Alloy metal

Blade Color:
Green

Focusing Crystal:
Single Adegan crystal

Notes

The Zabrak species from Iridonia tend to be a warlike
people with an aggressive culture, and though decades
of Jedi training turned Eeth Koth into a serene Jedi
Master, he designed his lightsaber hilt for assertive
combat. Eeth Koth, on occasion, entered into the
Concordance of Fealty, an ancient Jedi tradition in
which Jedi Masters swap lightsabers for an extended
period to more fully understand the ways in which Jedi
were bonded to their weapons.

Notes

Saesee Tiin used a common lightsaber handle
design shared by several of his fellow Jedi,
including Ki-Adi-Mundi and Aayla Secura.
However, Saesee's lightsaber shows a little
less wear than his colleagues'—not because
he was not a warrior, but because he was an
excellent pilot. For many of his missions, he
was behind the controls of a starfighter rather
than in the thick of personal combat.

Like those of other hilts, the ridges along the upper half of this handle support a two-handed style of combat. This hilt also possesses a locking switch to keep the blade active when thrown.

Hilt Length:
26.60 centimeters (10.50")

Hilt Width:
4.50 centimeters (1.80")

Material:
Alloy metal

Blade Color:
Green

Focusing Crystal:
Single Adegan crystal

This style of hilt includes a pair of flat adjustment dials. The uppermost dial controls the blade width, while the second dial switches the energy beam between a pair of focusing crystals.

Hilt Length:
26.60 centimeters (10.50")

Hilt Width:
3.30 centimeters (1.30")

Material:
Durasteel and brass

Blade Color:
Green and blue

Focusing Crystal:
Two Adegan crystals

Notes

Agen Kolar and his young Padawan learner Tan Yuster were two of the Jedi who accompanied Mace Windu on the mission to Geonosis that sparked the Clone Wars. Yuster died in combat, overwhelmed by superbattle droid forces. Kolar salvaged Yuster's lightsaber and removed the blue crystal from its handle, eventually adding it to his own as a secondary blade in a gesture to honor the memory of his apprentice.

Notes

Obi-Wan Kenobi constructed this lightsaber
after his promotion to the rank of Jedi Master
at the start of the Clone Wars, replacing
a model design that he had used since he
was a Padawan. (See pages 10 –11.) This
lightsaber was also the model from which
Luke Skywalker constructed and designed his
lightsaber. The gleaming metal alloy would
eventually become tarnished from almost two
decades of disuse amid the wastes of Tatooine.

The narrow neck along with the ribbing on the handgrip makes this distinctively Obi-Wan's lightsaber.

Hilt Length:
29.20 centimeters (11.50")

Hilt Width:
5.00 centimeters (2.00")

Material:
Alloy metal

Blade Color:
Blue

Focusing Crystal:
Single Adegan crystal

This sleek and elegantly designed hilt, composed of valuable metals, is much shorter than most lightsaber handles, which makes it easy to conceal.

Hilt Length:
19.00 centimeters (7.50")

Hilt Width:
5.00 centimeters (2.00")

Material:
Aurodium cap with phrik alloy casing

Blade Color:
Red

Focusing Crystal:
Single synthetic Sith crystal

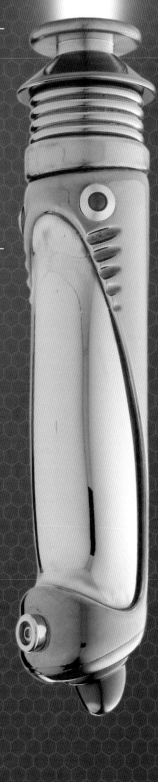

DARTH SIDIOUS
(A.K.A. THE EMPEROR)

Notes

The expense of the metals used to make this lightsaber mattered very little to someone with the wealth and authority of Darth Sidious in his day-to-day disguise as Chancellor Palpatine. Darth Sidious actually constructed at least two of these short-handled weapons. He kept one hidden within a neuranium sculpture in his executive office, and another tucked in his sleeve.

Similar in look to Anakin's first lightsaber (see pages 32–33), this gleaming hilt contains numerous additional technical interfaces, which grew out of Anakin's passion for tinkering with technology and engineering.

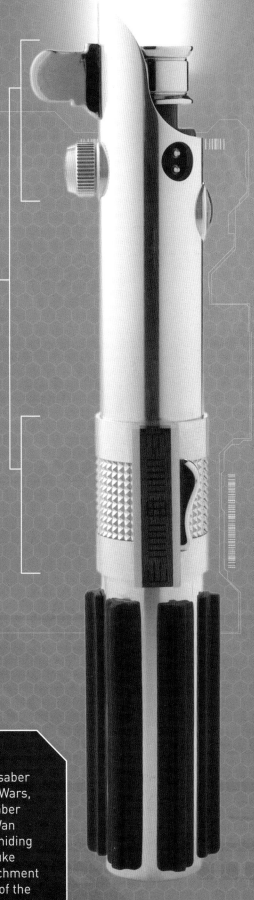

Hilt Length:
28.00 centimeters (11.00")

Hilt Width:
5.00 centimeters (2.00")

Material:
Alloy metal

Blade Color:
Blue

Focusing Crystal:
Single Adegan crystal

Notes

Anakin Skywalker created this lightsaber following the outbreak of the Clone Wars, but Obi-Wan Kenobi took the lightsaber after their battle on Mustafar. Obi-Wan kept the lightsaber while he was in hiding and, a generation later, gave it to Luke Skywalker. Luke felt an instant attachment to the lightsaber—the construction of the lightsaber and its crystals connected to him as it had to his father, Anakin.

DARTH VADER

Notes

Following his crippling defeat by Obi-Wan
Kenobi and then his painful rebirth as a
cybernetically enhanced Sith Lord, Darth Vader
was without a weapon. Thus Vader created a
hilt similar to that of his former lightsaber, but
with the characteristic red blade of the dark
side. He built the red blade by using a synthetic
crystal given to him by Darth Sidious.

Darth Vader's lightsaber resembles the one he carried as Jedi Knight Anakin Skywalker, but this design adds darker, heavier accents along its beam emitter, handgrip, and activation matrix.

Hilt Length:
28.00 centimeters (11.00")

Hilt Width:
6.30 centimeters (2.50")

Material:
Alloy metal and carbon composite

Blade Color: Red

Focusing Crystal:
Synthetic harmonizing Sith crystal

Inspired by Obi-Wan Kenobi's second lightsaber, this hilt features a ribbed handgrip and narrow neck.

Hilt Length:
28.00 centimeters (11.00")

Hilt Width:
5.00 centimeters (2.00")

Material:
Alloy metals and salvaged materials

Blade Color:
Green

Focusing Crystal:
Synthetic green crystal

LUKE SKYWALKER

Notes

After Luke lost both his father's lightsaber and his hand in battle with Darth Vader, he constructed a replacement from instructions found in the abandoned hut of Obi-Wan Kenobi on Tatooine. Luke's lightsaber strongly resembles that of his old Jedi mentor, but adds rings of cycling field energizers to give the lightsaber a stronger, more reliable blade.

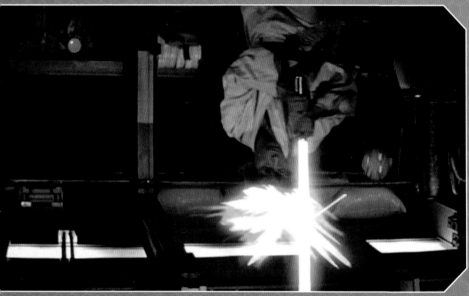

LIGHTSABER TECHNIQUES

Whenever possible, Jedi would prefer to outmaneuver or outthink their opponents, rather then rely on the power of the lightsaber. But that is not always possible, and Jedi must know how to use their lightsabers effectively.

Deflecting Blaster Fire

On the surface, it would seem foolish to bring a bladed weapon to a gunfight. However, the Force allows Jedi to exhibit supernatural reflexes that make it possible for them to block incoming blaster fire. A lightsaber blade is capable of deflecting a blaster bolt, and skilled Jedi can aim blasts back toward their enemies.

Long-range Attack

Most lightsabers incorporate a pressure activation lever that causes it to power down if dropped. They may also have a "lock" switch that keeps the blade active, so a Jedi can throw a lightsaber some distance and guide its path through the Force.

Cutting Through Obstacles

Beyond its use as a weapon or an instrument of meditation, a lightsaber is a practical tool. Given enough time, a lightsaber can cut through most substances. Even shield-rated blast doors will melt after extended exposure to a lightsaber blade, making it nearly impossible to imprison an armed Jedi Knight. Most Jedi will not risk slicing through bulkhead walls or high-energy force fields, though, because cutting into such a powerful source could be explosive.

MYTH
A lightsaber can cut through anything.

FACT
There are some materials that can withstand lightsaber contact. Phrik, a metal mined on the Gromas moon, cannot be cut by a lightsaber. Mandalorian iron, known as beskar, is also nearly indestructible. Some varieties of the metal cortosis have been known to deactivate a lightsaber upon contact. Thankfully for the Jedi, such exotic materials are too rare or costly to be widely used.

COMBAT

Lightsaber instructors have summarized thousands of years of combat techniques into seven basic forms, each with distinct philosophies, maneuvers, and defensive postures. Jedi Knights study multiple forms, but most tend to have a preference or strength in one.

Form I *Shii-Cho*: Determination

This is the most basic of all forms. It is taught to Jedi younglings as a foundation, and includes the fundamentals of stance, attack, parry, and landing a "Mark of Contact." Form I students practice through drills called *velocities*.

Form II *Makashi*: Contention

The maneuvers of Form II comprise a formal style of lightsaber-to-lightsaber combat. In the hands of the most skilled masters, the moves can be classical and elegant. It is difficult to penetrate the defenses—to injure, or damage, the weapon— of a true Form II master.

Form III *Soresu*: Resilience

This passive form emphasizes defense through efficient body movements, such as reducing the size of your target area. This form is best used to deflect blaster strikes.

Form IV *Ataru*: Aggression

A physically demanding style, this fighting form includes acrobatic jumps, flips, and weaves. It is truly the mark of a Force-skilled warrior to exhibit the amazing agility required by this form in combat.

Form V *Shien*: Perseverance

A more offensive version of the Form III style, this form uses techniques including the redirection of blaster strikes toward an opponent, or the use of defensive parries in order to force an attacker to drop his or her guard.

Form VI *Niman*: Moderation

This form seeks to balance the strengths of the previous forms through a combination of moderation and calm. A Jedi who has mastered Form VI wields amazing lightsaber skill, but does not focus on power or aggression.

Form VII *Juyo*: Ferocity

Also called *Vaapad*, this form is extremely dangerous and should only be attempted by the most disciplined Jedi Masters. It is a strong style of combat that requires intense energy. Such narrowed focus comes dangerously close to the aggressive instincts that surface from the dark side.

Target Zones

In basic lightsaber combat, an opponent's body is divided into six areas that form the six distinct target zones. These zones create a focus for training as well as attack during a lightsaber duel.

Zone 1 is the head, a lethal target that will end combat immediately.

Zone 2 is the right arm and side. **Zone 3** is the left arm and side. These areas can be the focus of attacks aimed at disarming an opponent.

Zone 4 is the midsection, or torso, but specifically refers to a target's back. Successful zone 4 strikes are almost always fatal.

Zone 5 is the right leg.

Zone 6 is the left leg.

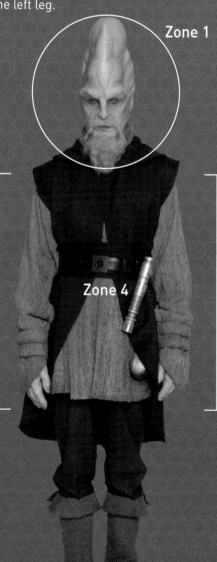

Zone 1

Zone 2

Zone 4

Zone 3

Zone 5

Zone 6

Jedi vs. Sith

This duel marked the first time Jedi and Sith lightsaber blades had crossed in centuries. Darth Maul's leaping assault nearly caught Qui-Gon Jinn off-guard. It was only through extreme focus that Qui-Gon was able to shake off any shock and put up a defense. However, if his escape vessel had not appeared in time, it is likely Qui-Gon would have tired under Darth Maul's relentless attacks.

||||||| | |||| ||||||| | ||||||||||| ||||||||||| |||| ||| || ||||| ||| | |||

A Padawan's Revenge

By separating the team of Obi-Wan Kenobi and Qui-Gon Jinn, Darth Maul was able to target each Jedi separately. He wore down Qui-Gon's defenses, and dispatched the Jedi Master with a quick jab to his chest. The act enraged Obi-Wan, who attacked Darth Maul in a rush. Though Obi-Wan's heated assault cut through the Sith Lord's double-ended lightsaber handle, it left him vulnerable to a sudden counterattack. Only by centering himself in the Force did Obi-Wan outleap the Sith Lord, and surprise Darth Maul with a swipe through the midsection.

NOTABLE LIGHTSABER DUELS

Duel on Geonosis

Anakin Skywalker and Obi-Wan Kenobi faced Count Dooku in an attempt to stop him from fleeing Geonosis. Dooku's Sith lightning blast briefly knocked out Anakin, allowing the Count to focus on Obi-Wan. Count Dooku's elegant use of Form II combat allowed him to slip past Obi-Wan's defenses and wound him on his arm and leg. Though Anakin recovered and forced Dooku back with a flurry of double-lightsaber strikes, Dooku slashed through Anakin's reckless assault and cut off his arm.

Duel of the Masters

With both younger Jedi fallen, Count Dooku seemed victorious. Yoda entered the chamber, however, to challenge the sword master. The two Force warriors attempted to defeat each other with displays of telekinesis and other Force abilities, but they were too evenly matched. They turned to their lightsabers, and with a masterful display of Form IV, Yoda dodged Dooku's attacks. Only when Dooku threatened the fallen Jedi was he able to distract Yoda long enough to escape.

Rematch Over Coruscant

Obi-Wan Kenobi and Anakin Skywalker faced Count Dooku again, this time aboard a Separatist flagship. Familiar with Obi-Wan's fighting style, the Dark Lord once again got the better of him. It was Anakin, at Chancellor Palpatine's command, who sliced through Dooku's hands and mortally wounded him to end the duel.

NOTABLE LIGHTSABER DUELS

Darth Sidious vs. Jedi Masters

When Mace Windu led a team of Jedi Masters to apprehend Darth
Sidious, none of them expected to face the power of the Sith Lord.
His innocent appearance as Chancellor Palpatine, along with an
application of a concentrated dark side confusion haze, enabled Darth
Sidious to take down Agen Kolar, Kit Fisto, and Saesee Tiin. This left
Mace Windu to battle the Sith Lord. Windu nearly overpowered Darth
Sidious, forcing him into a corner and holding him at blade point. It
was Anakin Skywalker who severed Mace Windu's arm, allowing Darth
Sidious to win the fight with a blast of Force lightning.

NOTABLE LIGHTSABER DUELS

Master vs. Apprentice

When it became clear that Anakin was lost to the dark side and had adopted the title Darth Vader, Obi-Wan was left with no option but to confront his former apprentice. Years of fighting side-by-side left these warriors evenly matched, and their exhausting duel crossed the fiery landscape of a Mustafar refinery. It was Anakin's overconfidence, fueled by the dark side, which led to his defeat. A mistimed leap over Obi-Wan allowed him to swiftly cut Anakin, leaving him disabled on the shore of a lava river.

The Circle Is Complete

A generation later, Obi-Wan Kenobi would face Darth Vader once again. While Vader wanted revenge, Obi-Wan was focused on buying time for his friends—including Luke Skywalker. Their duel was careful and measured compared to their previous meeting. Obi-Wan's movements were slowed by age and lack of practice; Darth Vader—recalling the grievous injuries he suffered during their last encounter—fought his former Master with apprehension, while his cybernetic body reduced his actions. Ultimately, Obi-Wan deliberately dropped his defenses, and Darth Vader cut through him, but the Jedi Master mysteriously vanished into the Force.

ULTIMATE LIGHTSABER DUELS

A New Jedi Hope

Although he had been only briefly instructed by Yoda, Luke Skywalker showed great ability in the Force during his duel with Darth Vader on Bespin. He had enough strength to challenge Vader, but Luke was far too hasty. The Dark Lord used telekinetic attacks and a shocking revelation to overpower the young Jedi. Darth Vader had already cut off his hand when he crushed Luke's spirit by revealing that he was in fact his father, Anakin Skywalker.

The Force Balanced

When Luke confronted Darth Vader again, he possessed the clarity and wisdom of a Jedi Knight. He had not set out to conquer but rather to redeem the good in his father. However, Vader, being carefully judged by Darth Sidious, enraged Luke by suggesting he would lure his sister, Leia, to the dark side of the Force. Luke lost his composure and attacked Vader. On the brink of the dark side, Luke let go of his anger. He resisted the Emperor's lure of power, and stood by his father. When the Emperor nearly killed Luke with an assault of Sith lightning, Darth Vader saved him by turning against the Sith Lord.